AF280946

William Beckford

DIE GESCHICHTE VON AL RAOUI

Eine Arabische Erzählung

DIE GESCHICHTE VON AL RAOUI

DIE

GESCHICHTE VON

AL RAOUI

EINE ARABISCHE

ERZÄHLUNG

Zum erstenmal ins Englische,
und aus dem Englischen ins
Teutsche übersetzt.

LONDON:

BEY C. GEISWEILER

1799

Wertheste Madame!

Es ist ein Gebrauch bey den Morgenländern, unter ihrem Gefolge einen Mann zu haben, dessen Pflicht es ist, Sie mit geistreichen Erzählungen zu unterhalten, *Al Raoui*, oder der *Märchen-Erzähler* ist der Titel, welchen sie ihm geben. Wenn diese Geschichte des Emirs, ein Meister in seiner Kunst, Ihnen einige Unterhaltung verschaffen kann, so wird es äußerst schmeichelschaft seyn für

den Uebersetzer.

In der Vorrede zu der *Geschichte von Vathek* wird einer Sammlung von Erzählungen erwähnet, wovon diese Geschichte eine ist. Es sind ohngefehr sechzehn Jahre, seit dem sie der Herausgeber übersetzte, und würde noch immer in Vergessenheit geblieben seyn; hätte nicht Major Ouseley in seiner sehr merkwürdigen Sammlung, genannt (*Oriental Collections*) eines Manuscripts, von welchem Hauptmann Scott Eigenthümer ist, Erwähnung gethan. Der Inhalt einer Erzählung, wie sie da mitgetheilt wird, erregte die Ueberzeugung von der Aechtheit der gegenwärtigen, oder wenigstens, daß sie eine große Aehnlichkeit mit jener habe. Denn es ist nöthig zu bemerken, daß von den Arabischen Erzählungen, von tausend und einer Nacht (*The Arabian Nights*) nicht zwey Manuscripte gefunden werden, die einander gleich sind. Würklich würde es sonderbar seyn, wenn es dem also wäre, denn ohne der Absicht der Person, die sie erzählt zu gedenken, so muß jede Geschichte in der Erzählung mehr, oder weniger Verschiedenheit haben.

Wenn der Hauptmann Scott, welcher vorzüglich die Fähigkeit besitzet, den Arabischen Erzählungen Gerechtigkeit wiederfahren zu lassen, sich geneigt zeigte, seine eigene Sammlung zu übersetzen, so würde er dadurch dem Publico eine Verbindlichkeit auflegen, welche es unmöglich ist mit Worten auszudrücken.

Herr Browne in seiner *Reise nach Africa, Egypten und Asia* die eben erschienen ist, thut eines Umstandes Erwähnung, welche da sie eine Stelle in der gegenwärtigen Erzählung erklärt, hier angeführt ist.

Wenn ein Befehl von Constantinopel ergehet – so werden die Stadhalter auf das Schloß vorgeladen um den Willen der Pforte zu vernehmen. Die so gegenwärtig sind, antworten so bald die Befehle gelesen sind, wie es der Gebrauch ist, *Esmana wa taâna*. Wir haben gehört und wir gehorchen.

Seit dem diese *Vorrede* nach der Druckerey geschickt wurde, findet sich daß Hauptmann Scott die Uebersetzung seines Manuscripts unternommen hat, und daß das *arabische Original* gegenwärtiger Erzählung in Major Ouseleys Morgenländischen Sammlungen (*Oriental Collections*) wird eingerückt werden.

Die Gesellschaft eines Emirs von Groß Cairo wurde einst mehr seiner Geistesgaben, als seines Ranges wegen gesucht. Eines Tages, da er sehr niedergeschlagen war, wand er sich zu einem seiner Hofleute, und sagte: Mein Herz ist schwer, und ich weis keine Ursache davon anzugeben; erzähle mir eine Geschichte, meinen Kummer zu zerstreuen. *Al Raoui* für den es genug war zu hören um zu gehorchen, antwortete: die Großen haben von jeher Erzählungen für das beste Gegengift des Kummers gehalten: wenn ihr mir es erlaubet, so will ich euch meine eigene Geschichte mittheilen.

In den Tagen meiner Jugend verliebte ich mich in eine der schönste Mädchen, welche die feinsten Gesichtszüge, und eine Haut rein wie Schnee hatte. Sie wohnte bey ihrem Vater, und ihrer Mutter, und ich, blos um sie zu sehen, gieng oft an ihrer Thüre vorbey. Als ich eines Tages, wie es meine Gewohnheit war, dahin gieng, und niemand zu Hause fand, fragte ich die Nachbarn, wohin die Familie gegangen wäre. Man sagte, sie hätte ihren Aufenthalt geändert, und wäre nach dem Lande der Camele gereiset, um da zu wohnen. Dieses betrübte mich im innern des Herzens. Unvermögend ohne das Mädchen zu leben, verlies ich alles, um ihren Wohnort aufzusuchen. Denselben Abend sattelte ich mein Camel, nahm mein Schwert, stieg auf, und trat meine Reise an.

Die Nacht war dunkel, der Weg beschwerlich, und mit Bergen, und Strömen durchkreuzt. Mein Elend zu vergrößern, fand ich mich von den Thieren der Wildniß umgeben. Oneracht allem diesem lobte ich den Herrn für alles, was da immer auch geschehen mögte, und setzte meinen Weg wie vorhin weiter fort. Ich ward von Ermüdung überwältiget, und der Schlaf bemächtigte sich meiner; ich unterlag seiner Gewalt, und schlummerte auf meinem Thiere ein. Während ich auf diese Art schlief, nahm mein Camel einen unrechten Weg; da es langsam fortgieng erwachte ich nicht, bis ich von dem Ast eines weitausgedehnten Baumes einen Schlag an meinen Kopf bekam. Als der Tag begann, durch den Schleier der Nacht zu brechen, nahm ich bey dem schwachen Schimmer der Morgen-Dämmerung wahr, daß ich merklich von meinem Wege abgekommen seyn müste. Wir vermögen nichts gegen den Willen Gottes! sagte ich zu mir selbst, wir müssen mit allem zufrieden seyn, was da geschiehet! Mit dergleichen Gedanken unterhielt ich mich selbst, und wande meine Augen nach allen Seiten; ich sahe die schönsten Gärten mit Bächen durchschlungen, und Vögel, die von der annahenden Morgenröthe erwecket, ihre süßesten Gesänge zu wirbeln anfiengen. Plötzlich stieg ich von meinem Camel, nahm es beim Zaum, und gieng zu Fuß, bis ich in das Land Alfla kam.

Hier hatte ich frischen Muth gefast, bestieg mein Thier, und da ich nicht wuste, in welcher Gegend ich wäre, überlies ich es der Führung des Himmels. Nachdem ich eine schöne Gegend durchgewandert hatte, fand ich mich abermahl an einer Wüste. Da beobachtete ich ein prächtiges Zelt, dessen ausgespannte Leinwand von einem blendenden Weiß, von dem Zefir des Morgens hin, und her gewehet wurde, und bemerkte zuweilen wie in einem Wetter-Strahl, dessen innere Pracht. Geiße und Kühe weideten umher; ein Camel und ein Pferd stand in der Nähe an ihrem Pfahl, aber kein menschliches Geschöpf erschien. Dies ist sehr sonderbar! sagte ich zu mir selbst. Endlich kam ich näher, und rief wer ist da? Bewohnt ein guter Muselmann dieses Zelt? Wolte er einem armen, verirten Reissenden auf seinem Wege zurecht weisen? Augenblicklich kam ein Jüngling hervor, schön wie der Mond, wenn er durch die Wolken bricht, und unter ihnen in die reine blaue Luft hervorblickt. Sein Anzug trug zur Gracie seines edlen Anstandes bey. Er begrüßte mich mit einem Tone voll Gefälligkeit, und sagte: Bruder Arabier, ihr scheinet euern Weg verlohren zu haben? Ich antwortete, ja, so ist es, und ich zweifle nicht, ihr werdet mich zurecht weisen. – Bruder, sagte er, der Weg ist schlecht, es regnet nun, die Nacht wird dunkel seyn; und in dieser Gegend sind viele wilde Thiere, steiget ab, ruhet bey mir aus, und morgen will ich euch euren Weg weisen.

Bey diesen Worten stieg ich ab. Er band mein Camel fest, gab ihm Futter, und wies mich in sein Zelt. Als ich niedergesessen war, verlies er mich, und gieng nach einem Schaafe. Nachdem es geschlachtet, und mit geschmackvollen Kräutern zubereitet war, setzten wir uns zu Tische. Während unserem Mahle seufzte der Jüngling öfter, und weinte. Ich vermuthete, daß Liebe die Quelle seiner Thränen sey, denn da ich selbst liebte, bemerkte ich leicht, daß er äußerst lieben müsse. Man weiß nicht eher, was Honig ist, bis man ihn gekostet hat. Ich wünschte von ihm den Zustand seines Herzens zu erfahren, fürchtete aber unbescheiden zu scheinen.

Als wir hinlänglich gegessen hatten, brachte er in einem goldenen Gefäß zwey Flaschen von Christal: eine mit Rossenwasser, die andere mit Wein, nebst einem Handtuch von Seide mit goldenen Franzen besetzt. Ich wusch meine Hände, und bewunderte die Pracht, und den Geschmack, mit welchem mein Wirth mir aufgewartet hatte. Wir unterhielten uns eine Weile miteinander, und nach diesem führte er mich in das innere seines Zeltes, zeigte mir eine reiche Matratze von grüner Seide, welche mit Vorhängen von derselben Farbe umgeben war, und verlies mich, nachdem er mir eine erquickende Nachtruhe gewünschet hatte. Ich legte meine Kleider ab, und fiel auf der Stelle in den Schlaf. Nie hatte ich eine süßere Ruhe genossen. Meine Einbildungskraft, erfüllt mit allem, was ich gesehen hatte, und meine Seele, eingewiegt von der Gastfreyheit, und dem Betragen meines Wirthes spiegelte mir Träume voll Vergnügens, und Friedens vor. Nach einigen Stunden Ruhe, ward ich von einer Stimme aufgeweckt, die harmonischer war als eine Flöte. Ich öfnete den Vorhang leise, und nahm nebst meinem Wirth eine junge Frauensperson gewahr, die schön war, wie die Erste der Houries. Einen Augenblick hernach hörte ich viel Geflüster. Anfänglich dachte ich, die Schönheit, welche ich gesehen hatte, sey eine Tochter der Genien, die sich in diesen Jüngling, verliebt habe, und sey hierher gezogen um seiner zu geniesen. Denn ihr Blick verbreitete einen Glanz, wie die Sonne auf jeden Gegenstand um sie her. Bald aber fand ich, daß sie eine Tochter Arabiens sey.

Da ich sah, daß sie sich beyde im hereinkommen bey der Hand nahmen, stelte ich mir leicht vor, daß sie sich liebten, und konnte nicht unterlassen, ihr Loos zu segnen. Ich zog augenblicklich meinen Vorhang zu, legte meinen Kopf auf mein Kissen, und fiel abermahl in einen Schlaf. Als ich mich des Morgens angezogen hatte, gieng ich, nachdem ich mich gewaschen, und mein Gebet verrichtet hatte, zu meinem Wirth. Wir nahmen unser Frühstück zusammen ein, aber ich unterlies, mich über das, was ich gesehen hatte, zu erkundigen. Nachdem unser Mahl vorüber war, sagt ich – Nun hoffe ich, eure Güte wird mir meinen Weg zeigen, wodurch alle schon empfangene Gunstbezeigungen einen neuen Zuwachs erhalten werden. Wisset, antworte er, daß es der Gebrauch der Araber ist, ihre Besuche auf drey Tage auszudehnen, überdies bin ich euch für eure Gesellschaft verbunden, und wenn es euch behagt, länger bey mir zu bleiben, wird es mich freuen. Seinem Verlangen Genüge zu leisten, und die drey Tage noch bey ihm zuzubringen, schien mir am besten. Während dieser Zeit, nahm ich jede Nacht wahr, daß das Mädchen zurückkam. Nach deren Verlauf konnte ich mich nicht länger enthalten, ihn zu fragen, wer er sey? Er antwortete, ich bin einer aus dem Geschlecht des Beni Asra*, nannte mir seinen Nahmen, und den Nahmen seines Vaters und jene der Brüder seines Vaters. Als ich dieselbe gehört hatte, wuste ich, daß er der Sohn meines Oheim sey, von dem großen Geschlecht des Beni Asra. Ich unterrichtete ihn hiervon, und sagte ferner: warum, mein Vetter, hast du dein erhabenes Haus verlassen, um in dieser Wüste allein zu wohnen? Kaum hatte ich diese Worte gesprochen, so erwiederte er – Ich kam, mein Vetter, in dieser Wüste zu wohnen, weil es der Auffenthalt meiner Geliebten ist. Ich liebe die Tochter meines Oheims des jüngeren Bruders meines Vaters. Ich verlangte sie von ihrem Vater, er aber versagte sie mir, und verlobte sie an einen andern, auch einen Verwandten, welcher nachdem er mir ihr verbunden war sie nach seinem Wohnsitz brachte. Während eines Jahres war ich meiner selbst nicht bewust, und da es mir unmöglich war, von ihr entfernt zu leben verlies ich alles und kam hierher. Sie die meine Seele liebt, wohnt am Fusse jenes Berges, und kommt jeden Abend, eine Stunde, mit mir zuzubringen. Um diesen Trost zu geniesen, bleibe ich hier an dieser Stelle, und hoffe, daß durch Gottes Hülfe alles gut gehen werde. – Dann sagte ich, wenn sie diesen Abend kommt, und du willst sie auf mein Camel setzen, nimm alles, was du von Werth hast mit dir, und kommt beyde mit mir. Der Schritt meines Thieres ist so schnell, daß ihr vor dem Anbruch des Tages fern von hier seyn werdet. Alsdenn sollst du, ohne daß dich jemand hindert, das Vergnügen genießen, bey deiner Geliebten zu seyn, und es soll dir zugleich freystehen, deinen Wohnsitz aufzuschlagen, wo es dir behaget, denn das Land Gottes ist sehr groß, und so viel ich vermag, will ich dir in allem behülflich seyn. Mein Vorschlag gefiel ihm, und er nahm ihn mit besonderer Zufriedenheit an. Wir erwarteten mit Ungedult, bis der Abend herannahe, um zu hören, was das Mädchen sagen würde.

Beim Eintritt der Abenddämmerung giengen wir nach der Thür, und sahen ihrer Ankunft mit voller Erwartung entgegen. Jedes Geräusch schien uns den

Tritt ihres Fusses zu verkündigen. Er bestrebte sich ihren Wohlgeruch von der Luft einzuathmen. Wir warteten mit Besorgniß so lange vergebens, daß mein Vetter mit zitternder Stimme ausbrach. Ein Unglück muß sie auf dem Wege betroffen haben! Erwarte hier meine Rückkunft, ich will gehen, nach ihr zu sehen. Indem er dies gesagt hatte, gieng er in das Zelt, nahm sein Schwert, und eilte von dannen.

Nach Verlauf von zwey Stunden kam er zurück, und brachte ein Bündel unter seinem Arme. Todtenblässe deckte sein Angesicht, zitternd, und verstöhrt eilte er auf mich zu, und indem er fallen ließ was er gebracht hatte, sank er unbeweglich zu meinen Füssen. Nach einer Weile schien Leben in ihm zurück zu kehren, aber seine Ohnmacht wich nur, um den bittersten Klagen Plaz zu machen. In Verzweiflung schrie er endlich aus – Ein Löwe überfiel – zeriß meine Geliebte! Sieh! Hier ihr Gewand, ihr Schleier, und ihr Blut! Hier ist nun alles, was von ihr übrig geblieben ist. Als er dieses gesprochen hatte, blieb er eine Stunde in einer Verzuckung, und heftete seine Blicke in einem sprachlosen Starren auf ihre Kleidung. Dann schien er weniger wild, und sagte: – Bleib! Ich gehe aus, werde aber bald wiederkommen.

Nach einer Stunde kam er in das Zelt zurück. – Er hatte den Kopf des Löwen in seiner Hand, warf ihn auf den Boden, verlangte Wasser von mir, und nachdem er das gerunnene Blut davon gewaschen hatte, küßte er dessen Mund. Seine Thränen flossen nun aufs neue. Er blickte mit starrem Auge auf den Gegenstand des Schreckens, welcher bis jetzo in einen Theil ihrer Kleidung eingewickelt war, und brach in einen gräßlichen Seufzer aus, der mein Herz durchbohrte.

Ich nahete mich ihm, er ergriff meine Hand, und sagte! Ich beschwöre dich bey der Liebe unserer Verwandte – bey der Freundschaft, welche wir einander zugeschworen haben, diese Begebenheit für unsern Anverwandten geheim zu halten. Laß es nie über deine Lippen kommen. Möge das Gedächtniß meines Unglücks sowohl, als meine Glückseligkeit – so kurz in ihrer Dauer – immer mit mir hier in Vergessenheit begraben liegen. Ich werde bald aufhören zu seyn.

Wenn ich todt bin, wasche mich, kleide mich mit der Kleidung meiner Geliebten, und begrabe mich mit dem was von ihr übrig ist unter den Eingang dieses Zeltes. Alles was es enthält, ist dein: Mögest du es in größerem Glücke genießen, als ich! Auf diese Worte begab er sich in die innerste Abtheilung des Zeltes. Nach einer Stunde kam er zurück; sank auf den Boden, drückte meine Hand und verschied.

Bestürzt über den Anblick wünschte ich mir anfänglich den Tod; Ich erinnerte mich aber dessen, was er mir anempfohlen hatte. Nachdem ich ihn gewaschen, begrub ich ihn seinem Willen gemäs, und blieb drey Tage an seinem Grab zu weinen. Denn kehrte ich voll von Betrübniß über diesen traurigen Zufall – statt nach dem Lande der Camele zu reisen, nach dem Ort meines vorigen Aufenthalts zurück.

Denn das Unglück, von welchem ich so eben
Zeuge gewesen ware – hatte mich
gänzlich von Liebe
geheilet.

THE STORY OF AL RAOUI

THE STORY OF

AL RAOUI

A TALE FROM THE

ARABIC

LONDON:

Printed by C. Whittingham, Dean Street, Fetter Lane

FOR C. GEISWEILER PALL MALL

Sold also by G. G. and J. Robinson, and H. D. Symonds,
Paternoster-Row; J. Richardson, Royal Exchange;
G. C. Keil, Magdeburg; B. G. Hoffman,
Hamburg; G. J. Goeschen, and
J. G. Beygang, Leipzig.

1799

My Dear Madam,

 it is usual with the Easterns to retain an Attendant, for the sake of amusing them with ingenious recitals; and *Al Raoui*, or *The Taleteller*, is the title they give him. If this Story of the Emir's, an adept in his art, can afford You any amusement, it will be highly gratifying to   The Translator.

In the Preface to *The History of Vathek*, a collection of Tales is mentioned, of which this Story is one. It was translated above sixteen years since, and still would have remained in oblivion, but for notices of a manuscript possessed by Captain Scott, which occur in Major Ouseley's very curious *Collections*. The contents of a Tale, as there expressed, suggested the persuasion of its identity with this; or, at least, of its being very similar to it: for, of *The Arabian Nights*, it deserves to be remarked, that no two transcripts are found to be the same. Indeed, it would be strange if they were; for, setting aside design in the person reciting them, each Tale in recital must, more or less, vary.

If Captain Scott, who is preeminently qualified to render them justice, could be induced to translate his own collection, it is impossible to say how great an obligation, he, by it, would confer on the public.

Mr. Browne, in his *Travels in Africa, Egypt and Asia*, just published, mentions a circumstance, which, as illustrating a remark in the following Story, is for that reasons subjoined.

When a firmân or mandate is received in Egypt from Constantinople, the Beys are summoned to the castle to hear the commands of the Porte. Those who attend, as soon as the reading is finished, answer, as is usual, *Esmana wa taâna*, 'We have heard, and we obey.'

Since the foregoing *Preface* was sent to the press, it is found, that Captain Scott has undertaken the translation of his Manuscript; and that the *original Arabic* of this Tale; will be inserted from it, in Major Ouseley's *Collections*.

There was formerly an Emir of Grand Cairo, whose company was more sought for his genius, than his rank. One day, being very sad, he turned to an attendant and said: my heart is dejected, and I know not the cause; relate to me some story, to dissipate my grief. *Al Raoui*, with whom hearing was obedience, replied: the Great deem stories an antidote to chagrin; if you will allow me, I will tell you mine own.

In the days of my youth, I became enamoured of a beautiful damsel, who, with symmetry of features, had a skin pure as snow. She dwelt with her father and mother, and I, only to behold her, often passed by their door. Going thither one day, as was my custom, and finding no one within, I asked of their neighbours, whither they were gone? – It was told me, they had changed their habitation, and were departed, to dwell in the Valley of Camels. This greatly afflicted my heart. Not able to live any longer without her, I relinquished my all, to seek her abode. What evening, I saddled my camel, girded on my sabre, mounted the beast, and set forth.

The night was dark, the road difficult, and perplexed by precipices and torrents. To increase my distress, I was surrounded by the howlings of the desert. Notwithstanding, I blessed God for whatever might occur, and went on as before. At length, dropping with fatigue, drowsiness oppressed me; and, subdued by its power, I dozed as I rode. Whilst thus slumbering, my camel went astray; but, proceeding slowly, I did not awake, till my forehead was stricken by the branch of a tree. As day was beginning to dawn, I discerned by the faint glimmering, that I had wandered widely from my way. We cannot go against God's will! said I to myself; we must be content with whatever may happen! Reasoning in this manner, I turned my eyes on all sides, and beheld pleasant gardens divided by streams, and birds that, incited by the beams of the morning, harmoniously blended their sweetest songs. Instantly alighting, I took my camel by the bridle, and walked onward, till I entered the land of Alfla.

Having thus recovered spirits, I remounted my beast, and not knowing whither I was come, entirely resigned her to the guidance of God. After crossing a delightful region, I found myself again on a wild. There, I beheld a magnificent tent, whose awnings, of dazzling white, were waved by the breath of the morning; and, at glimpses, discovered the splendour within. Goats and sheep were pasturing round; a camel and horse stood near at their picket, but no human creature appeared. – This is very strange! said I to myself. At length, approaching, I called: Who is there? – doth not some good Mussulman inhabit this tent? – would he point out his way to a traveller bewildered? Immediately came forth a youth, beautiful as the moon when, leaving a cloud, she stoops from beneath it, into clear blue sky. His dress gave a grace to his noble appearance. He saluted me with the accent of gentleness, and said: brother Arab, you seem to have erred from your road? – I answered that I had, and trust you will guide me. – Brother, said he, the tracks hence are imperfect, it now raineth, the night will be dark, and, in this region, are many wild beasts: alight, rest yourself with me; and, to-morrow, I will point out your way. At these words I dismounted. Tying up my camel, he gave her some provender, and ushered me into his tent. When there seated, he left me, and departed in search of a sheep. Having killed and prepared it with savoury herbs, we placed ourselves at his table. The young man, during this repast, ceased not to sigh and to weep. I divined that, from love, proceeded his tears; because, my-self, being conscious of love, I judged he must love vehemently: for one knows not what honey is till we taste it. I wished to learn from him the state of his heart, but feared to appear indiscreet.

When we had sufficiently eaten, he brought out, in a golden canteen, two bottles of chrystal, one with musked rose-water, the other with wine; and a nap-kin of silk, bordered with gold. I washed my hands, admiring at the magnificence and taste that my host had displayed. We then conversed for a while, after which he introduced me to the interiour of his tent, shewed me a rich matrass of green silk, furnished with curtains of the colour; and retired, wishing me refreshment from slumber. I undressed myself, and sunk at once into sleep. Never did I enjoy a more tranquil repose. My imagination possessed by what I had seen, and my soul soothed by the hospitality and deportment of my host, presented to me dreams of pleasantness and peace. After some hours of rest, I was wakened by a voice, more melodious than a lute. Softly drawing back the curtain, I discovered with mine host a young woman, lovely as the chief of the Houries. After a moment, I heard much whispering. Methought, at first, the Beauty I saw was a daughter of the Genii in love with this youth, and sequestered here to enjoy him; for her look cast a radiance, like that of the sun, upon every object around: but I soon found her no other than a daughter of Arabia.

Seeing them hand in hand, as they entered, I easily perceived they were lovers; and could not refrain from blessing their lot. Immediately closing the curtains, I reposed my head on the pillow, and again yielded to sleep. In the morning, having put on my clothes, after ablution and prayer, I went to mine host. We broke our fast together, but I asked no question of what I had seen. When our meal was ended, I said: Now, hope I your kindness will shew me my way; it will be a favour conferred upon all that are passed. Know, replied he, it is a custom with the Arabs to lengthen their visits to the end of three days; moreover, your company is acceptable to me, and I shall rejoice if it please you to stay. Finding myself constrained to fulfil his desire, I tarried with mine host till the fourth day came, and saw, each night, the damsel return. At the end of this time, I forbore, no longer, to ask him, who he might be? – He replied, I am one of the tribe of Beni Azra*; then told me his name, the name of his father, and his father's brethren. On hearing these names, I knew him to be the son of my uncle, of the great tribe of Beni Azra. Of this I apprized him, and further inquired: Why, my kinsman, hast thou forsaken thy illustrious house, to dwell alone in this desert? – No sooner hat I spoken these words, than he answered: I came, my cousin, to dwell in this desert, it being the abode of her whom I love. I am enamoured of the daughter of my uncle, the second brother of my father; I sought her at his hands, but he denied my request, and betrothed her forthwith to another, our kinsman, who, having gone in to her, led her away, to the place where he himself dwells. For the space of a year I was not myself, and being unable to live from her sight, I abandoned all to come hither. She whom my soul loveth, abides at the foot of yond mountain, and every evening returns, to converse for an hour with me. It is for this comfort that here I remain; and trust, by God's favour, all will be well. – Then, said I, if, when she shall come this evening, thou wilt scat her on my camel, take what thou hast which is precious, and go together with me; the foot of my beast is so fleet that, before the day can dawn, we shall be far removed from this place. Then wilt thou enjoy, without any to hinder, the solace of abiding with her whom thou lovest; and thou shalt be free to choose the abode of thine eyes; for the land of God is very wide: I also will help thee, to the utmost of my power. – This proposal pleased him well. He embraced it with a look of delight. We waited impatiently till evening should come, to hear what the damsel would say.

When twilight drew on, we repaired to the door, earnestly expecting to see her approach. Each air seemed to bring the tread of her step. Her perfume, he tried to inhale from the breeze. After anxiously waiting a long time in vain, my kinsman, he cried, in a faultering voice, some misfortune most surely hath beset her on the way! Abide my return; I will go forth to see. – On saying this, he entered the tent, snatched up his sabre, and went.

In the space ot two hours I saw him come back, with a bundle pressed under his arm. His visage was covered with the paleness of death. Trembling and be-wildered, he hurried towards me, and, dropping what he brought, fell, lifeless, at my feet. After some time, he appeared again to revive, but his faintness gave way to the bitterest anguish. At length, in distraction, he loudly exclaimed: a lion hath met, hath devoured my beloved! – lo! her robe, her vail, and her blood! – Here, is all of her now that remains! – Having thus spoken, he continued for an hour, entranced, and speechless, gazed on her vestments. Then, looking less wildly, he said: – Remain! – I am going, but soon shall return.

Within another hour he re-entered the tent, bearing in his hand the head of the lion. This, casting on the ground, he asked me for water, and, having washed off the gore, he kissed its mouth. His tears, now, gushed forth afresh, and, beholding with stedfastness the object of horror, till then muffled up in a wrap of her dress, he uttered a groan that cleft through my heart.

I approached; he grasped my hand, and said: I conjure thee, by the love of our kinswoman; by the friendship we have mutually sworn, to keep this adventure undivulged to our kin; let it not depart from thy lips. May the memory of my misfortune, as well as my felicity – so short in duration! – be for ever buried in oblivion. I shall soon be no more. When I am dead, wash me: put on me the robe of my beloved, and inter me, with her remains, in the door of this tent. All it contains is thine. Mayest thou enjoy it more happily than I! – At these words he retired to the inmost apartment: – in another hour coming forth, he sunk upon the earth, compressed my hands, and expired.

Amazed at the sight, I, at first, wished for death, but soon recollected the injunctions he had given. Having washed, I interred him, according to his will; and tarried three days to lament by his grave. Then, full of affliction from this woeful event, instead of proceeding to the Valley of Camels, I returned to the place of my former abode; for the evil, thus witnessed, had healed me of love.

VERSES

The Verses which follow, were long ago printed;
    but with more defects than their own.
They are here annexed, for the sake of correcting them.

VERSES

By the side of the stream that strays thro' the grove,
I met in a ramble the blithe God of love;
His bow o'ver his shoulder was carelessly tied,
His quiver in negligence clank'd at his side;
A grasp-full of arrows he held to my view,
Each wing'd with a feather, that differ'd in hue.
This, fledg'd from the eagle, he smiling begun,
I aim at the heart that no danger will shun;
And this, from the peacock, all gaudy, array'd,
The breast of Sir Fopling is sure to invade:
When I aim at the prattler, who talks, void of wit,
My shaft in the plume of a parrot will hit;
And when I've a mind that the jealous should smart,
An owl-feather'd arrow will pierce through his heart.
For the youth in whom truth and fondness reside,
From the breast of a dove my dart is supply'd;
This I value the most: – and this 't was, I found,
From you, O my Delia, that gave me the wound.

CONJUGAL LOVE

AN ELEGY

If aught of bliss sincere hath e'er been giv'n,
   To those who dwell so far beneath the skies,
That bliss, which makes on earth a present heav'n,
   Can only from the purest passion rise.

Say, do not storms uproot the lofty oak,
   That crowns with majesty the mountain's brow;
While lowly shrubs escape the thunder's stroke,
   And wave their verdure in the vale below?

Say, does that soil whose bosom gold contains,
   From its rich lap in more profusion throw,
Or sweeter flow'rs than scent unpillag'd plains,
   Where baneful gold hath ne'er been taught to glow?

Say, does that haughty bird whose gaudy train
   Attracts the full gaze of the splendid day,
Pour from the heart so soothing, sweet a strain,
   As modest Philomela's melting lay?

Ambition, av'rice, and the pomp of pride,
   Seductive oft, may lure unheedful eyes,
But ne'er can tempt my right-on foot aside;
   These who pursue, will ne'er obtain the prize.

Remote from envy, far from madding strife,
　　I nothing want, of competence possess'd;
Amid the scenes of mild domestic life,
　　I'll seek, by blessing others, to be bless'd.

Be mine the first, the most endearing care,
　　That nought may e'er disturb my Delia's joy:
Whate'er to her could cause the lightest fear,
　　Would instant all my happiness destroy.

For her I'd wake e'en at the glimpse of dawn,
　　And blithsome at the heavy plough would toil;
Anticipating, e'er my wish'd return,
　　The ready welcome of an heart-felt smile.

When autumn o'er our fields her produce spreads,
　　And vying reapers bend in adverse rows;
With pleasure she the yellow landscape treads,
　　And wipes the dews of labour from their brows.

Should sickness e'er molest my menial train,
　　With lenient hand she 'd ev'ry grief assuage;
Her sympathy would draw the sting of pain,
　　Revive the young, and charm e'en wayward age.

Should some kind friend frequent our humble shed,
　　With studious ease she 'd grace the frugal board;
Before our guest her rural treasures spread,
　　Nor boast a treat but what our grounds afford.

Should some bewilder'd trav'ler as he strays,
　　Protection seek beneath our shelt'ring roof,
For him she'll make the cheerful hearth to blaze,
　　Of hospitality the promptest proof.

The hallow'd raptures of the bridal bed,
    When, first entranc'd, we seal'd our mutual vow,
Transport less poignant through the bosom sped,
    Than yields the fond delight that fills us now.

Ah, speak, my Delia, thy o'erflowing heart,
    When, cradl'd in thine arm, the tender boy,
With filial smile doth first begin t' impart,
    He knows his mother, source of all his joy!

Or, when around my knees the infant band,
    In clamb'ring contest seek the envy'd kiss,
Impetuous, each extends the pleading hand,
    T'assert his claim, and all obtain the bliss;

While we, in sportive contest, strive to trace,
    In which each parent's semblance most prevails,
Their father's vigour and thy winning grace,
    In varied mixture o'er each feature steals.

Oft, when their little tongues but ill can tell
    The sprightly fancies in their brain that rise;
With keen attention thou explor'st them well,
    And read'st the meaning in their speaking eyes.

'Delightful task, the tender thought to rear,
    To teach the young idea how to shoot!'
To prune each impulse that a vice might bear,
    And tend with fos'tring hand the rip'ning fruit!

When tott'ring lambkins, from the searching air,
    Unable yet the fresh world to sustain,
Demand the fold, be their's the tender care,
    Nor will they hear the suff'rers bleat in vain.

When timid read-breast, pinch'd by taming cold,
　　Enters our friendly cot in search of food;
Be their's the joy to make the stranger bold,
　　And learn the luxury of doing good.

Thus, with their op'ning minds our pleasures spread,
　　While they in all that's just and gen'rous thrive,
Till autumn's mellowing hues our days o'ershade,
　　Then in our scyons we'll again revive.

Fond mem'ry then shall make us feel anew,
　　Those happy hours, when you first touch'd my heart;
Recall each dear idea to our view,
　　When you that wounded, smiling eas'd the smart.

Then, in my boys, some lovely maid I'll woo,
　　Whose virtues, and whose form, resemble thine;
While, in your girls, shall pay his court to you,
　　Some honest youth, whose bosom glows like mine.

And when, at length, draws on the gloom of death,
　　We'll praise our God for all his blessings giv'n;
In gentle slumber yield our easy breath,
　　And, both transported, wake to bliss in heav'n.

WRITTEN, IN THE CLOSE OF WINTER,

TO

A FRIEND

JUST LEAVING A FAVOURITE RETIREMENT,
PREVIOUS TO SETTLING ABROAD.

Ere yet your footsteps quit the place
Your presence long hath deign'd to grace,
With soft'ning eye and heart deplore,
The conscious scenes, your own no more.

When vernal clouds their influence show'r,
Expand the bud, and rear the flow'r,
Who to yond leafing grove will come,
When the rath primrose loves to bloom,
And fondly seek, with heedful tread,
The forward floret's downy head?
Or, when the vi'let leaves the ground,
Scent the pure perfume breathing round?
The garden tribes that gladlier grew,
While cherish'd by your fost'ring view,
No more disclose their wonted hues,
No more their wonted sweets diffuse!

Who first will spy the swallow's wing?
Or hear the cuckoo greet the spring?
Unmark'd shall then th' assiduous dove,
With ruffling plumage, urge his love;

Unnoted, though in lengthen'd strain,
The bashful nightingale complain!
O'er the wide heath who then delight,
Led by the lapwing's devious flight,
To see her run, and hear her cry,
Most clam'rous with least danger nigh!

Who, saunt'ring oft, will listless stay,
Where rusticks spread th' unwither'd hay,
And, o'er the field, survey askance
The wavy vapour quiv'ring dance?
Or, sunk supine, with musing eye,
Listen the hum of noon-day fly?
Or watch the bee from bell to bell,
Where shelter'd lilies edge the dell?
Or, mid the sultry heat reclin'd,
Beneath the poplar woo the wind?
While, to the lightest air that strays,
Each leaf ist hoary side displays.

Who, drawn by nature's varying face,
O'er heav'n the gath'ring tempest trace?
Or, in the rear of sunny rain,
Admire the wide bow's gorgeous train,
Till, blended, all its tincts decay,
And the dimm'd vision fleets away,
In misty streams of ruddy glow,
That cast an amber shine below;
And, melting into ether blue,
The freshen'd verdure gild anew!

Who now ascend the upland lawn,
When morning tines the kindling dawn,
To view the goss'mer pearl'd with dew,
That glist'ring shoots each mingling hue?
Or mark the clouds in liveries gay
Precede the radiant orb of day?
Who, when his amplest course is run,
Wistful pursue the sinking sun?
To common eyes he vainly shines;
Unheeded rises, or declines!

In vain with saffron light o'erspread,
Yond summit lifts ist verdant head,
Defining clear each whiten'd cote,
And tuft of copse, to eye remote;
While, down the side-long steep, each oak,
Outbraving still the wood-man's stroke,
Detains, athwart th' impurpling haze,
A golden glance of west'ring rays.

The rook-lov'd groves, and grange between;
Dark hedge-row elms, with meadows green;
The grey church, peeping half through trees;
Slopes waving corn, as wills the breeze;
The podding bean-field, strip'd with balks;
The hurdl'd sheep-fold; hoof-trod walks;
The road that winds aslant the down;
The yellow furze-brake; fallow brown;
The wind-mill's scarcely circling vane;
The villager's returning wain;

The orient window's crimson blaze,
Obtrusive flaring on the gaze;
The eager heifer's echoing low,
Far from her calf compell'd to go;
From topmost ash the throstle's lay,
Bidding farewell to parting day;
The dale's blue smokes that curling rise;
The toil-free hind that homeward hies;
The stilly hum from glimmering wood;
The lulling lapse of distant flood;
The whitening mist that widening spreads,
As winds the brook adown the meads;
The plank and rail that bridge the stram;
The rising full-moon's umber'd gleam,
'Twixt sev'ring clouds that, richly dight,
Let gradual forth her bright'ning light;
No more the onward foot beguile,
Where pollards rude protect the stile.

Whose look now scans the dusky sphere,
To note succeeding stars appear?
Who now the flushing dawn descries,
That upward streams o'er northern skies?
Or the wan meteor's lurid light,
That, headlong trailing, mocks the sight?

Mid the lush grass, who now require
The glow-worm's ineffectual fire?
Or catch the bells from distant vale,
That load by fits the fresh'ning gale,
Till flurry'd from her ivy'd spray,
The moping owl rewing her way?

When autumn sere the copse invades,
No more you haunt the wood-land glades,
To eye the change from bough to bough;
Or eddying leaf descending slow,
That, lighting near her calm retreat,
Prompts the shy hare to shift her seat;
Or, peering squirrel nimbly glean
Each nut that hung before unseen;
Or, flitting down from thistle born;
Or, glossy haw that crowds the thorn,
Whence, oft in saws, observers old
Portend the length of winter's cold!

Wak'd by the flail's redoubling sound,
When spangling hoar-frost crisps the ground,
No more forego bewild'ring sleep,
To climp with health yond airy steep!
When deep'ning snows oppress the plain
The birds no more their boon obtain;
The red-breast, hov'ring round your doors,
No more the stated mess implores!
Where all that needed found relief,
No tearful eye laments their grief;
No lenient hand dispels their pain;
Fainting they sue, yet sue in vain.

But though the scenes you now deplore,
With heart and eye, be your's no more;
Though now each long known object seem
Unreal, as the morning's dream;

You still with retrospective glance,
Or rapt in some poetic trance,
At will, may ev'ry charm renew;
Each smiling prospect still review:
Through mem'ry's power and fancy's aid,
The pictur'd phantoms ne'er shall fade.
And, oh! where'er your footsteps roam,
Where'er you fix your future home,
May joys attending crown the past,
And heav'n's best mansion be yor last!

FINIS

* Beni Asra ist ein arabischer Volksstamm, von welchem die mehrfach dichterisch verwertete Sage geht, daß sterben müsse, wer unter ihnen von der Leidenschaft der Liebe erfaßt werde. / Beni Azra is an Arab tribe of which a legend says that he, among them, who is suffering from love is deemed to die.

Die englische Übersetzung der Geschichte von Al Raoui *und die Gedichte werden mittlerweile Samuel Henley zugeschrieben. Da diese Ausgabe aber dazu dienen soll, die Geschichte wieder zugänglich zu machen, fiel die Entscheidung zugunsten des bekannten Autorennamen aus. / The English translation of* The Story of Al Raoui *and the Verses are now ascribed to Samuel Henley. For the intention of this edition is to bring this story back into print and to make it available again, it is published by the name with which it is associated.*

In der deutschen Übersetzung wie im englischen Original sind selbst offensichtliche Fehler in Schreibung und Interpunktion beibehalten worden. Die einzigen Korrekturen sind typographischer Art – Punkte hinter Titeln und Überschriften wurden entfernt und Auszeichnungen im deutschen und englischen Text vereinheitlicht. / Even obvious spelling and punctuation errors have been retained. The only corrections are of typographic nature – periods have been removed from titles, and italicising has been unified.

Titelfotografie / Cover Photograph: *Sahara* von Rudolf Lehnert

William Beckford:
Die Geschichte von Al Raoui. Eine arabische Erzählung
Hrsg.: Saskia van de Kraats
Herstellung und Verlag:
Books on Demand GmbH, Norderstedt
ISBN 3-8334-4405-3

Bibliografische Information Der Deutschen Bibliothek. Die Deutsche Bibliothek ver-
zeichnet diese Publikation in der Deutschen Nationalbibliografie; detaillierte bibliografische Daten sind im Internet über http://dnb.ddb.de abrufbar. / Bibliographic
information published by Die Deutsche Bibliothek. Die Deutsche Bibliothek lists
this publication in the Deutsche Nationalbibliografie; detailed bibliographic data are
available online at http://dnb.ddb.de.